THE

LITTLE

QUEEN

~ the little queen ~

written by
MEIA GEDDES

illustrated by
SARA ZIEVE MILLER

 Poetose Press

ISBN 978-1-945366-66-6 (paperback)

ISBN 978-1-945366-23-9 (e-book)

Library of Congress Control Number: 2016946722

Published by Poetose Press

Printed in the United States of America

First Edition

Cover and illustrations by Sara Zieve Miller

CONTENTS

I.   Wherein a little girl becomes a little
      queen 1

II.   Wherein the little queen embarks on
      an adventure 4

III. Wherein the little queen climbs
      another hill not her own 12

IV.   Wherein the little queen encounters
      bugs, brushes, and brooms 18

V.   Wherein the little queen walks up
      the Ladder to Heaven 24

VI.   Wherein the little queen begins to
      learn the language of her world 26

VII. Wherein the little queen makes her
      way to the Main Market 27

VIII. Wherein the little queen considers
      the worlds offered by windows 32

IX.   Wherein the little queen speaks of
      loss 37

X.   Wherein the little queen finds that
      vulnerability may come in many
      forms 41

XI.   Wherein the little queen receives the
      sleep she has said she needs 45

XII. Wherein the little queen embarks on
      a second adventure 49

XIII.   Wherein the little queen joins a
board of directors 57

XIV.   Wherein the little queen feels an
infinite ache and offers the sound of
her smile 61

XV.   Wherein the little queen embarks
on a third adventure with great
determination 68

XVI.   Wherein the little queen has a
frighteningly ecstatic realization 74

XVII.   Wherein the little queen discovers
more foreign languages 78

XVIII.   Wherein the little queen seeks a gift
in the Jungles 82

XIX.   Wherein the Happening happens 88

XX.   Wherein the little queen wanders
and walks 90

XXI.   Wherein the little queen reflects in
the Wild Rose Gardens 93

XXII.   Wherein the little queen makes use
of a little piece of string 98

XXIII.   Wherein the little queen and her
friends make homes for those in
need 102

XXIV.   Wherein nothing much remains
to be said 109

THE

LITTLE

QUEEN

- I -

Wherein a little girl becomes a little queen

On a little world, upon a little hill, a little tear fell down a little face. A little girl was now a little queen.

The little queen's mother and father had said that she would live on, for a long time, and that her tears would magnify the life around her forever more, but they had not explained how she should go about going on.

The little queen placed the plump shapes of her tears in a glass jar and watched the jar fill up, day after day. She stood by two gravestones enveloped by roses and placed her palms on trees and wondered questions that could not be answered. She returned to her palace squeezing roses in her palms and let her small breaths fog the windows as she looked down on the happenings happening below her hill.

The little queen lived in a world where the sky swirled like the sea and nothing was itself for very long. Everything looked to be in brushstrokes. Walking along, she often felt she could paint herself into the canvas of the world in whatever way she might want.

Yet for many months, the little queen moved slowly, making only the smallest strokes, as if she was simply trying to stay on the canvas. She watched her jar of floating tears fill up and held it close to her heart. She brought it to the roses on the gravestones and watered them well.

One day, the little queen took a long look at her jar and a long look at her salty roses. The jar was full and the roses were dying. The palace was empty and she was very much alone.

The little queen did not know what to do or where to go. Perhaps most importantly, she did not know who to be, for it occurred to her that she did not really wish to be a little queen. She believed there were better things to be.

That is why, on this particular day, sitting among her salty roses, she decided that she should see the world. Maybe she would find someone who would like to take her place as little queen. After all, she thought, maybe others would like to feel what it is to be a queen, even if just a little one. And that is how the little queen embarked on an adventure.

- II -

Wherein the little queen embarks on an adventure

Walking beyond her palace and down her hill, the little queen found herself overwhelmed by many new sights and smells. She did not know what to see or smell first. But it was easy enough to know when she saw the light. It was a great glass dome, an orb of library light. Indeed, the roof of the library looked to be an enormous page, soft and warmed by the sun. The inside was illuminated by the pretty print of millions of books.

The library's librarians did not pay any mind to the little queen as she wandered inside. She made her way forward, letting the dark cool created by the many books embrace her. She thought of the dark cool of her palace and how different this dark cool of the library felt in comparison. Each book seemed to call her forth, and the scent of aged pages seemed to hug her from all sides.

She breathed in deeply. She wondered what the smell of book tears might be like.

Maybe dust, she thought.

As she went on, dipping her head into many aisles and many books, the little queen felt as though she were emerging from something wonderful over and over again. It was a terrifying feeling, to continue, because she did not want it to end. But eventually, of course, she came upon the book sniffer, as most visitors do if they delve into the depths of a library.

The book sniffer stood in a lightless aisle sniffing books. She paid no mind to the little queen. After a moment, the little queen made a polite little grunt. The book sniffer smiled and walked toward the little queen, nose wiggling and yearning toward the books all around.

The book sniffer's assignment was to sniff the books, ensure that all smelt as they should. Each day, she took in a deep breath, let one out in exchange, and forgot to stop. She inhaled these fields of books waiting to be smelled, imagined each little space for each little letter. Lights would gleam through book spines, illuminating cover edges.

"Ah," the little queen said, as if she had smelt a book for the very first time. "I would love to be a book sniffer," she said. "I am the little queen, if you would like to trade places with me."

"It takes training to become a book sniffer," the book sniffer replied kindly. Her nose wiggled and turned as she spoke, just like her eyes, and it seemed that she had sacrificed some amount of sight for the sake of discerning scent.

The little queen was about to admit that being a little queen did not take much training when an approaching rustle caught their attention. "Who is there?" the book sniffer called out.

Out of the depths of the aisle came a voice. "I am the wall sawyer," the wall sawyer said. The wall sawyer carried a large saw in her hands.

"I am the book sniffer," the book sniffer replied.

The wall sawyer did not ask the little queen what she did. This was because in the little queen's kingdom, people only volunteered their doings if they wanted to, and they never asked others their doings. It was considered impolite. Asking what one did was like asking who they were, and that was too simple a question for a very complex answer.

The little queen did not mind not being asked what she did, for she really did not know what she would say.

"I wonder how we might shape the flow of space in the world through walls," the wall sawyer said. "I know I am a wall sawyer, but there are times that walls are what create the right space."

"Like these walls of books," the book sniffer proposed.

"They do affect the concentration of the air," the wall sawyer admitted.

"I wonder—what is the perfect confluence of all the world's smells?" the book sniffer asked. The book sniffer seemed to have a marvelous idea. She smiled so that her nose widened in a beautiful way. "With your walls and my nose, we could work together to determine that," she suggested.

"Tomorrow we shall conduct test cases and determine the perfect confluence of all the scents of the world," the wall sawyer announced.

"My nose is salivating," the book sniffer said.

Then the conversation was over as abruptly as it had begun, but everyone understood and went on their way. The book sniffer continued sniffing, the wall sawyer left, and the little queen followed the wall sawyer.

The little queen wanted to ask the wall sawyer a question, though she felt rather uncomfortable doing so. She did not have much experience with the whole business of asking questions, even though her father had excelled at it. They had often played a game in which he would ask her all the questions that he could think of. She would provide lengthy answers and he would always take her at her word. He liked to say he was proud to have a daughter who knew everything.

The little queen wanted to ask the wall sawyer how she had become a wall sawyer, but knew that this question was considered a rude one. She was so curious, however, that she asked it anyway, in a small voice: "Excuse me, but how did you come to be a wall sawyer, if you do not mind my asking."

To her relief, the wall sawyer smiled and embarked on a lengthy explanation.

She had decided to become a wall sawyer, shaping space, when she realized that all good places offer sufficient space to breathe. Without the obstruction of walls, one could ambulate to and fro. One could breathe free. Lives were widened. Great things happened in open hibernacula of space. Echoes and air could communicate. Cutting down a wall, the wall sawyer could feel the tension in a home ease and something windy rush in circles round her feet. It was addictive, each a sweet victory of art. The tumbling motion of a falling wall was like a volcanic eruption fading into a mountain of roses. The wall sawyer felt a loving animosity toward walls. "You must pay attention to your obsessions, where life and love intersect," she told the little queen.

Again, the little queen felt an overwhelming sense of discovery. *So this is what it is supposed to feel like*, she thought. "I am the little queen," she said, "but I do not know how to be any kind of queen. Would you like to be the little queen in my place?"

The wall sawyer shook her head. "You will make a great little queen," she said. "As for me, I may not want to saw walls all my life, but this is what feels right at this moment in time."

The little queen nodded, for she had thought the wall sawyer would say something like this. She thanked the wall sawyer and went on her way, wondering what obsessions she might adopt that day.

The little queen thought about who she would like to be. Some would say she was a royal rose or the daughter of a queen, but she knew she was more than a flower, and definitely not simply a daughter. She did not even know if she liked her name. But it would have to do for now.

Leaving the library, when the little queen looked back at her palace, all she saw now was a brown speck on a purple hill. It was a hill shrouded in lavender, the kind with long stalks and a velvety feel. She sighed and let her eyes sink into the color. The lavender and its green leaves created swirling patterns from a distance. She did not allow herself to look for long, and walked on.

III

Wherein the little queen
climbs another hill not her own

The little queen decided to climb another hill, any hill but her own. As she went along, she thought back to her salty roses and remembered something her mother had spoken of: the rose petal poet, a lady who wrote poems on rose petals and gave them away. They were legendary poems. It was not long before people believed that the rose petal poet's poems taught a person how to be. The little queen thought it would be lovely to meet the rose petal poet and to read such poems. Maybe she could find her.

The little queen did not come across the rose petal poet at the next hill, but she did come upon the tree woman—or rather a woman trying to be a tree, standing very still.

It was a little sad because the woman did not have any leaves. She only held them in her palms and hair.

"Why are you pretending to be something you are not?" the little queen asked the tree woman.

"I can be whomever I wish to be, and I wish to be a tree," the tree woman said, extending a leaf to the little queen. The little queen accepted it with thanks.

The tree woman had legs of birch and curls such that bees would lose themselves in each small curve. She reminded the little queen of her beautiful mother, strong and delicate, obstinate and free.

The tree woman had wanted to be a tree since youth. Each day, her stomach a cacophony of knots, she trembled to the park and, arms aloft, thought she felt the squirrels, birds, and wind form her limbs to bark, find a home in her locks and legs. When the birds began to nest, she would not leave. At each day's close, she sought the next eagerly. She thought to be a tree was to be in the best aspect, for in the early morning there came a sliver of time in which everything was a beginning, a rebirth after dreams.

The little queen looked at the tree woman for many moments. She seemed to glow like she held the sun close.

The little queen was not the only one entranced. People traveled long distances to meet and feed the tree woman, her mouth spread wide to receive food. All these people stood around her now in a crowd, including the leaf gluer.

"Maybe this business of being a tree is a manageable thing after all," the leaf gluer said to herself quietly. The little queen looked at the leaf gluer looking at the tree woman's long limbs and at the tree woman looking at the leaf gluer's long fingers.

"My dear, it is not so easy to be a tree, not at all," the tree woman said. "Yet I can be little else," she added, addressing the gathered crowd.

"I too cannot deny myself," the leaf gluer said.

"It is the time I can concentrate on being me the most," the tree woman said. "And I feel much closer to others as a tree. I like when the birds nest in my hair and the squirrels store nuts in my pockets."

"Perhaps you would like some leaves," the leaf gluer offered.

The leaf gluer loved the touch of autumn, the taste of fall's sweet breeze, her mouth wide open, gulping all of it in. She followed leaves, their journeys up and down and all around to

no known end but earth's soft soil. At autumn's close, it seemed she did not understand that all things come to end. Each and every day she took a leaf and placed it quite strategically upon the ground or in a tree so fall never would end. With eyes like blue-green worlds, she glued these leaves with an attentiveness that would fix the earth. Her leaves were works of art, crinkling color nestled in empty lanes and barren trees. People came to see her leaves from all around the world, though never saw what they had planned to see. After all a leaf is just a leaf and glue will hold for just a wee-long while till dust and rain and snow.

"Oh my," the tree woman sighed. "I would love to have some leaves, but I am afraid I could not pay for your services."

"I would be honored to leaf you for free," the leaf gluer offered.

"This is a very good day turned better," the tree woman said.

The little queen caught a glimpse of a shiver rushing through the body of the tree woman as the leaf gluer began leafing her, drawing from her large pockets full of leaves.

The leaves fit the tree woman perfectly. The leaf gluer knew her art.

"Have you ever made a park of leaves?" the tree woman asked as she was fitted with leaves. "It could have decaying leaf labyrinths and leaf statues," she added.

"A lovely idea," the leaf gluer said.

"I definitely will come see the Park of Leaves

when it is complete," the tree woman said.

The leaf gluer nodded. "Hopefully, when you visit the Park of Leaves, it will not yet be dust."

"A Park of Leaf Dust is another idea," the tree woman said.

"Yes, there is nothing like sun mixed with floating dust," the leaf gluer agreed.

The little queen smiled at this thought. She went on her way, hoping to see dust floating on sunbeams that day. She wished that she could think of such ideas as the Park of Leaves or the Park of Leaf Dust. She did not know why she liked these ideas so much, but as she walked on, she imagined little spirals of leaves and dust and sun fading in and out like memories.

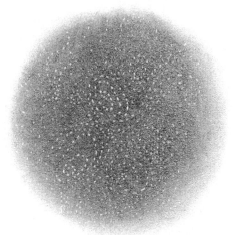

IV

Wherein the little queen
encounters bugs, brushes, and brooms

T he little queen would not see dust floating on sunbeams that day, but she would come upon the sun resting in a field of poppies, which is just as magical. In this field of poppies at the top of the next hill, she glimpsed a tiny tower edged with sky. In the window of this tiny tower was the outline of a small, sitting person.

Perhaps it was the rose petal poet hard at work, lovingly leaning over each petal with a needle squeezed between her fingers. Or maybe it was a poppy petal poet. Anyhow, this small person reminded the little queen of herself, sitting at the window of her palace awaiting the possibility of a miracle.

At this thought, the little queen's stomach trembled. Moving forward, though, focusing on her walk, she approached the tiny tower's door. She knocked.

A smiling voice welcomed her inside.

The little queen felt she had stumbled upon an entirely new experience of orange. This was the famed canvas of the seasons painter, a canvas thick with glistening orange paint, a field of poppies for day or night, a work with layers of paint that measured nine fine inches wide.

The little queen had heard of the seasons painter, but never had she understood just how much paint could be on a canvas at once and how orange a room could feel. The seasons painter depicted the seasons with paints of cadmium orange and cerulean blue, Prussian green and burnt sienna. No one knew that she also had slipped a face in here or there among the shadows, dappled dots of sunlight flitting through the leaves of trees. Within each layer, she also painted herself, a contour of crepuscular sun looking down on things from the top left corner.

The little queen stood beside the seasons painter, busy painting the creature sweeper passing by outside the window. She listened to them converse.

"You sweep a lot," the seasons painter said.

"You sit a lot," the creature sweeper said.

"I paint each day," the seasons painter said.

"Tomorrow is the same as this day," the creature sweeper said, still sweeping.

"You know you cannot keep every bug away," the seasons painter said, still painting.

The seasons painter swooshed her brush and the creature sweeper swooshed her broom.

The creature sweeper kept paths clear of creatures treading feet might crush. Moving like a brisk cloud, she never stood in the same place twice. Those who caught a glimpse of the creature sweeper sweeping by marveled at the passing frenzy of arms and legs, but did not know that at times she felt she was the only one who cared to sweep the world.

"Perhaps you ought to try a different kind of broom, maybe a brush," the seasons painter said.

"The bugs might like the brush," the creature sweeper replied.

The little queen browsed the seasons painter's many brushes. One had an end almost the size

of a broom. She pointed at it, and the seasons painter nodded, then opened the window to offer the brush to the creature sweeper.

"Thank you," the creature sweeper said.

"What do you think?" the seasons painter asked.

"Come and see," the creature sweeper responded.

The seasons painter hesitated. She had only to complete another half of a leaf and she thought the painting would be done for the day.

The creature sweeper called again, and that decided things. The seasons painter and the little queen went outside.

"You have swept me up as well, in a kind of way," the seasons painter said, joining the creature sweeper. The little queen stood off to the side. When the seasons painter saw the work her brush had done, she nodded in approval. "Very nice," she said.

"I think so," the creature sweeper replied.

The little queen looked upon the seasons painter and the creature sweeper and thought that for a moment, the two formed a kind of painting.

The seasons painter came over to the little queen, then, and slipped the little queen a brush from her back pocket. "You too may find a brush useful at times," she smiled. The little queen nodded in surprise. Then everyone nodded goodbye.

The little queen found herself once again on her own. She stood on the swept path and wondered at herself. She felt that she was not really the little queen, as if she did not fit the shape of what a little queen should be.

She thought about what all her adventures

would come to. She had read stories in which the heroes embarked on journeys and returned home changed, though she did not know if things were going the way they were supposed to go. She did not have the training to be a book sniffer or a wall sawyer. She did not have the patience to be a tree woman or a leaf gluer. She did not have the dedication to be a seasons painter or a creature sweeper.

It occurred to her that she was like that great orange canvas of paint, a great many layers of person. She needed to add a few layers here and there, to sweep herself up a bit. If only she were half a leaf from done.

*Wherein the little queen
walks up the Ladder to Heaven*

By and by, the little queen came upon the Ladder to Heaven, a stretch of road that crept up the east-facing side of a hill and fell down its west-facing side. The Ladder to Heaven was a famous street painted by a renowned street painter. People loved to say that those who reached the peak of the Ladder to Heaven always found the journey down to earth most sweet, and that each of the street painter's streets was just such a thing.

Walking up the Ladder to Heaven, the little queen felt her spirits rising with the setting of the sun. She said hello to a few bugs. She began to sing, low and long, and she thought of those she loved. When she reached the top of the hill, she began to sob.

The little queen was not sure why she was sobbing, but she could not seem to stop.

That is when the animal singer came along. The animal singer sang that she would sing a song, then began to sing in time to the little queen's sobs. She sang and sang. For after all, the little queen was an animal, a little animal wondering where in the world she was. The animal singer sang songs the little queen did not know. They were gentle, melodious songs with foreign words and filled the little queen with something sweet like hope. For a song will always find a way to fit into an animal's body, including that of a little queen.

When the sun had fully set, the animal singer left the little queen to her dreams. The little queen slept, quiet and resting, bathed in moonlight. Tomorrow, she would walk down the Ladder to Heaven back to earth.

Wherein the little queen
begins to learn the language of her world

When the little queen awoke the next morning, she sang to the bugs at her feet, and breathed in color. She rose and passed roses, chirping birds, and trees. And as she walked along, it occurred to her that maybe the rose petal poet had been her mother. Maybe she would have to make her own slips of rose petal poems.

When the little queen moved her hands through air and earth and swung her legs forward in long, steady strides, she felt a tingling. Lying in fields, she looked up at the sky and thought how the clouds looked like clusters of stars and how the stars looked like tiny suns. Climbing trees, she looked down at the earth and thought how everything moved in slow swirls of color. It all looked so beautiful. The little queen did not realize that she was learning the language of her world.

The little queen wandered so far that when she peered into the lakes she passed, she no longer could see her palace. She did not know her way, but once she had gotten started it was easy enough. She followed the Main River to the Main Sea, then following the Main Sea, she reached the Main Market.

The Main Market stretched along the Main Sea so buyers and sellers could easily transport their wares. It was a happening place, and folks from all regions passed through each day. There were rows of tables and tents full of marvelous things.

As she wandered, pondering, the little queen came across a whispering crowd. The crowd was spread across a crag overlooking the sea. As she approached, the little queen heard talk of a dream writer. She thought how fitting it was to stand like this on a crag among sky and earth and sea, just as in a dream. She stood with the crowd observing the woman sitting at her desk writing.

Suffice to say, the dream writer had a way of phrasing things. She could depict the curve of a cucumber, the shape of a sunbeam, the endearing, velvety tilt of a peach, in just such a way that she earned her living selling dreams. One simply made a selection, read it in solitude, and let it percolate till sleep. People swore they fell directly into her renderings, and one even asked if the dream writer could write a dream of dreaming forever. The dream writer could not do this, but she hired dream apprentices to expand the reach of her dreams and she wrote dreams for herself in which she would sit at a desk, pen in hand, and write even more dreams. This nearly doubled her output.

The little queen felt that she ought to buy a dream, though the wait looked to be very long. Also, there was one woman who seemed particularly eager to speak to the dream writer, pushing ahead of all others.

"I need to buy a dream," the woman said, almost shouting.

"Do you have any experience with dreams?" the dream writer asked in a soft voice. Everyone leaned forward, for the rush of the sea below was too loud at the moment for such an important conversation.

The woman sighed, for she would have to speak for her dream. "Of course I have experience with dreams. I am the dream counter. A dream is the realest thing there is. It is alive. It is a being. It can haunt a life," she said.

"Go on," the dream writer replied. The dream writer was not particularly inclined to sell the dreams she wrote, for they sold themselves if they were the right dream for the right person.

"I seek release from a terrible dream," the dream counter explained.

"How long should this dream be? What shape should it take? What mood would be right?" the dream writer asked.

"It must be a beautiful dream that transcends all other dreams," the dream counter said. "It must be a huge dream, a dream of almost unimaginable scope," she continued. "It must have the tint of flowers just as the sun rises on a spring day in the country, the wind carrying the rooster's crow and the chicken's cluck and the vibrating space between two fields separated by a road," she concluded.

"You have an intuition for this dream it seems," the dream writer said, smiling.

"I have thought long and hard about this dream and the dreams I want to leave," the dream counter said. The little queen wondered whether one truly could leave dreams behind.

"Why do you not write this dream yourself?" the dream writer asked. The little queen and the crowd leaned forward, and it occurred to the little queen that if this conversation got any more interesting they all would fall into the sea.

"I did not know I could write it," the dream counter said. She paused. Then she told the crowd about herself.

The dream counter had always been a counter, for she wondered about numbers. How many tons of ink had accumulated upon all the pages of time, for instance. She wanted to know the number of silences in a moment, to measure the life in a breath, to count candelas in the luminosity of shadows. But the most pressing question of all was the number of dreams one had in a night of sleep.

"Writing a dream is simple," the dream writer said. She withdrew a sheet of paper from her pocket. "This is a dream I wrote," she said, handing it to the dream counter. "A dream of writing dreams."

The dream counter looked at the sheet of paper, the crowd peering over her shoulder. The page was filled to the edges with words.

"Now you see, dreams are always present in their seeming absence—you just need to find them and coax them out," the dream writer said, addressing everyone, her eyes wandering over to the little queen.

The dream writer continued in this vein, and the little queen walked on, immersed in thought. She could not remember any of her dreams and resolved to mind them more from now on. And perhaps, she thought, she would try to write a few.

VIII

*Wherein the little queen
considers the worlds offered by windows*

It was not long before the little queen spotted someone she recognized among the faces in the Main Market crowd.

The little queen knew the window builder because this woman had built the windows of the little queen's palace when she was a child. She had taught the little queen to see windows in the strangest places, like in the space between someone's gaze and the ground. What days those had been!

The window builder had taught the little queen to love a good window. The window builder's windows let a person peer from one space into another. Her windows could be as little as a cup or as large as a small pond. They could be as thick as bricks or as thin as skin. She loved a great curving window that wrapped around a house and a miniscule peephole enveloped by a door. She loved the windows of sky between the branches of trees and the window of a bright shining hole within a wall. She made all kinds of windows wherever she went.

As the little queen approached, she joined a crowd immersed in a conversation between the window builder and another woman. It was not long before it became clear that this woman was the window counter, though the little queen was unsure what a window counter did. *Maybe she is like the dream counter*, she thought.

"How many windows might you build for me in a day?" the window counter asked in an urgent voice.

"I cannot build windows that fast," the window builder said.

"How long does it take to build a window?" the window counter persisted.

"I suppose a month to a day," the window builder said.

The window counter frowned. "You just said you could not build a window in a day."

"You seemed in such a rush, I think I simply could not keep up with the conversation," the window builder said.

"Alright, what do I do first?" the window counter asked, staring at the window builder.

"First one looks around," the window builder said, smiling. She waved at the little queen, then, and the little queen waved back. "To build windows is to see the spaces that want to be seen," the window builder announced.

"Maybe certain things do not want to be seen," the window counter said. She sighed. Then she addressed the crowd.

The window counter considered numbers often. How many tons of air did the universe contain, for instance. She wanted to know the average number of thoughts projected on an object in its life, to measure the silences in a dream, to calculate the ideal amount of light a window should emit. But the most pressing question of all was the number of windows the world contained. How many worlds could a person view from within or without?

The window counter once believed she saw a very sad sight through her bedroom window. After this, she wanted to fill her mind with windows of other things and beings. She wanted to know the number of worlds that availed themselves to her, a number only one who counted windows could ever know.

The crowd murmured in empathy. The little queen longed to wrap her arms around the window counter to console her. She thought how alike the window counter and the dream counter seemed, and wondered if they were friends. Maybe she could introduce them. There was a silence. Then the window builder announced, "I long to create a roomful of windows."

"Like a big glass ball?" the window counter asked.

"Like a big glass ball of many windows, including windows within windows," the window builder said.

The window counter smiled, for this is what she longed for as well. "Let us begin immediately," she said.

The little queen thought about all the windows she had at her palace and how she had better begin using them. She felt an inexplicable excitement at the thought of going home to write some dreams and discover some windows. There were so many pieces of paper waiting to be filled up and so many windows waiting to be found.

IX

Wherein the little queen speaks of loss

The market was such a happening place that the little queen felt she must take the opportunity to gather up all the knowledge she could. Then, she would be able to put together all this knowledge and know how to go about being a little queen.

When the little queen came upon a conversation in which the participants seemed particularly excited, she paused. She was finding that she could learn from those who were passionate about their doings and these two seemed very animated.

The lotioner and the plant whisperer spoke so softly that the little queen had to lean forward to better hear them. When they noticed her standing there, they paused and introduced themselves. Then they returned to their heated discussion without further ado. The little queen joined in too.

The three looked rather funny standing in a triangle leaning in toward one another. It did not help things when the rain began, a pitter-patter so soft it felt like snow.

"The application, the form, the shape of the act—it is all a craft," the lotioner said.

"Yes," the plant whisperer whispered. She could whisper many things that only someone who whispers plants into being would know. With hands as cool as leaves, she let her whispers spread out like water.

"What do you think will happen when you, a great whisperer, die?" the lotioner asked.

"This conversation is turning dark very quickly," the plant whisperer whispered.

"Do you want to know what I think of death?" the lotioner asked.

"Do I?" the plant whisperer whispered.

The little queen listened with bated breath, the rain sliding down her cheeks and nose. A few tears came out, too, but she did not notice them.

"I think it will be just like the moment after your whisper," the lotioner said. She paused dramatically. "A moment of release and expectation," she said.

Perhaps, the little queen thought. She sighed. She felt like she was part of a secret that needed to breathe a bit, like dry skin and leaves. "I'm not sure," she said without thinking.

"Oh, I am probably wrong, but I like to pretend to myself that I am right to see how it feels," the lotioner said.

"Ah," the little queen said. Then she explained, slowly, "I lost two people very dear to me . . ." She trailed off, then. She could not go on, only let the rain and tears fall down her cheeks.

The lotioner and the plant whisperer held out their hands, then, for holding. The little queen took them and felt her own being squeezed in return. Their hands were soft, like lotion and leaves.

They stood for a long moment. Then, the little queen said, "I am the little queen. It is very nice to meet you. Please feel free to come to my palace if you ever need. Now, I will go on." Her new friends nodded.

The little queen quietly stepped away. She felt a little bit more like a little queen, now. She did not know it, but as the lotioner and the plant whisperer watched her walk on, they felt glad to know they had a little queen.

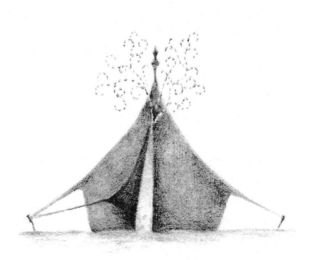

- X -

Wherein the little queen
finds that vulnerability may come in many forms

The little queen smelled something wonderful. It was the sweetest merging of wet earth, warm skin, and the gentlest of scents. It came from a nearby tent that drew her irresistibly . . .

The perfumer's tent made the little queen feel free to breathe in an odd sort of way. The perfumer dealt in perfumes of a certain sort. It was when, in the unfortunate presence of multiple nostril witnesses, someone discharged a big and nasty fart—the kind that percolates for a long while, growing many hours old—that the perfumer arrived. The perfumer tracked the borborygmi of these impending moments so that she more often than not arrived in time to offset the casualties. Cleansing the air, placing a spray or two here or there, the perfumer always brought sighs of relief.

The little queen was exploring one corner of the tent when a voice said to the perfumer, "Pardon my saying so, but a fart seems like a rather strange situation to get yourself mixed up in." This voiced precisely what the little queen was thinking. The voice came from the foreshadowing artist.

"A person who has farted can feel they are in a very vulnerable position," the perfumer said.

"Ah, I also try to help such folk," the foreshadowing artist said. Then she explained her work.

People came to ask her what they ought to do, what the future held. But she knew that only fools would give an answer, so she used her rolls of paper, pencils, paints, and pens to shadow in the different lines those lives could make. When her clients came to see the finished work, she spread her sheets upon the ground before them. They could go any direction they chose, but often they simply stood in awe of all the endless paths that one might take, as if awakened after a long while. It was as if the skies of their lives became easy to look at, cloudy or in sunset, beautiful and bursting. Standing there with them, she would say that she never could know that which would always be infinite, but that she always had thought her mind was meant to meander—this was the way it had meandered through their lives, but just this day.

"Perhaps your clients also could smell their way forward," the perfumer said. "I have always wanted to craft a line of experiential perfumes."

"A narration of smells, an adventure of subtle and exacting odors," the foreshadowing artist said.

The little queen looked at the perfumer and foreshadowing artist. They would be great leaders, for they could predict the future. "I suppose you two are not interested in being little queen?" she asked, but somehow she knew what the answer would be.

"Hah!" they laughed. "We would make terrible little queens," they both admitted. "But we are happy to advise," they added.

"Thank you! Your advice would be most welcome," the little queen replied.

The little queen took a deep breath and imagined life as pure possibility. She walked around the tent and thought how life could be like a song or a dream, a scent or a picture. It was all so lovely and tiring. The rain fell against the tent in a rough rhythm that made her heart feel like resting.

"I need to go to sleep," the little queen announced to nobody in particular.

"I can help with that," someone responded, from a neighboring tent.

XI

Wherein the little queen receives
the sleep she has said she needs

The sleep soother led the little queen to a long container close to the ground. The little queen sleepily wondered if it was a coffin. She lay down in the container-that-looked-like-a-coffin and the sleep soother placed a glass top over her. As the rain pounded against the glass top, the little queen listened to the sleep soother explain how she had come to sooth people to sleep.

"You see," the sleep soother began, "it was almost as if I had sleep in store, to be pulled from the pockets of my overalls." With her large hands and deep voice, the sleep soother could sooth one to sleep and soft dreams. She could rub the heads of folk weary from a long day's work and paint the night with lavender and chamomile. She could infuse light with dark and warm air with cool. But more often than not she simply sat and was still, waiting and waiting for sleep to come, though she never waited long. Sleep seemed to like her or maybe she liked it more than some. Often, simply sitting alone, the sleep soother would put herself to sleep unintentionally.

The little queen was fast asleep by the close of the sleep soother's explanation. She dreamt of letters written on air, petals merged with leaf, whispers met with scent, brushes made of page, and dreams that perfectly fit each window.

Upon waking, she saw a thousand droplets of water lit by the sun and heard the most curious voice in the distance. When she lifted the top off her container-that-looked-like-a-coffin, she heard the voice more clearly. She sat up and listened, then leaned back down out of sight. It was a voice one could listen to all day.

The poop encourager was saying that although she always had excelled at motivational speaking, she had never thought that encouraging people to finish a poop would be the right fit for her skill set. Yet she found she enjoyed this vocation, for she engaged in many excellent conversations.

The little queen was fascinated to hear that the poop encourager had a collection of various methodologies involving the production of sound, scents, jokes, riddles, and stories of differing tints. The little queen was very glad to have announced her need for sleep and for it to have led to this moment, now.

"Mostly, my patrons appreciate . . . my voice," the poop encourager said. "I suppose there is something about my voice that . . . moves . . . their bowels," she added. The poop encourager said she had never failed to help a person finish a poop, and of that she was proud.

The sleep soother's voice arose, then. "Alas, I have a client who cannot seem to sleep whatever I do," she said.

The little queen sat up, curious.

The poop encourager spoke slowly. "You might think it strange . . . but I have observed that when people get a whiff of what is below they tend to . . . go."

"They are encouraged by themselves," the sleep soother said.

"There is a . . . confirmation . . . that they have initiated . . . the act," the poop encourager said. "You cannot stop what has started."

"Yes! People can be very inspired by themselves," the sleep soother agreed.

"It is a good thing too because these are things one needs to do one's entire life," the poop encourager said.

At this point in the conversation, the little queen realized she needed to find a toilet. She had been too busy thinking about matters like life and death and how to live and such. She had forgotten how much she liked a good toilet.

And so, arising, she thanked the sleep soother, nodded to the poop encourager, and went on her way.

XII

Wherein the little queen
embarks on a second adventure

This was the day of The Long Book Race, so there were many opportunities to acquaint oneself with a toilet along the entirety of the route. The little queen promptly found one and dealt with the practicalities of life.

Everyone in the little queen's kingdom knew the story of The Long Book Race. The Long Book Race began because a woman known as the maker of long books once made a book half a mile long, a book she called *Long Book I*. She never thought anyone would bother reading *Long Book I*, but people loved this book so much that she decided to write *Long Book II* as part of a Long Book series. People loved *Long Book II* as much as they loved *Long Book I*. And so the maker of long books decided to put on a race for the release of *Long Book III*, which would complete the series. This race was the first in the world to combine a test of physical prowess with that of reading comprehension. *Long Book III* had long letters so participants could read and run simultaneously. They would turn the pages as they read and ran by grabbing hold of the handle at each page's end.

The little queen stood at the side of The Long Book Race feeling the whoosh of paper as a page flew by. A vague scent of text and sweat infused her body. She joined the crowd in cheering, making loud, encouraging sounds because no one was allowed to say words, which could distract participants.

A woman standing beside the little queen cheered with particular gusto. The little queen noticed this woman because she had string wrapped all around her body. Yet despite this, she seemed quite free. In fact, she was slipping and sliding in place with delight.

"Hello," the little queen said, though not too loudly to distract.

"Hello, I am the string woman," the woman responded.

"I am the little queen," the little queen said.

"Oh, I did not know we had a little queen," the string woman said. "It is a pleasure to meet you. Would you like some string?" She promptly cut a bit of string for the little queen and the little queen tucked it into her pocket with brush and leaf.

The string woman explained that she was wrapping a string around the world. She had partnered with the maker of long books so that the race and her journey would overlap. This helped the publisher of the long books save money, as their guards could join forces. At the moment, the string woman was taking a short rest from her journey to watch the race, which was particularly interesting because it had just rained.

The string woman looked at the little queen with interest. The little queen could see that the string woman wanted to know what she did as the little queen. "I am not really sure how to explain what a little queen does," she said apologetically.

"Well, there is nothing like doing something over and over again to know it more intimately," the string woman said.

"Like walking and walking with string," the little queen said.

"Yes, or like writing and writing, or running and running," the string woman said.

"Or living and living," the little queen suggested.

"I am not sure about that one," the string woman replied.

"Why?" the little queen asked.

"Walking and writing and running are very purposeful activities, but living we just happen to do regardless," the string woman said.

"Oh," the little queen said.

"Or not," the string woman said.

"Oh?" the little queen said.

"Well, maybe we can live in a particular way that makes things different than just living," the string woman said. "Maybe we can *live*, live, if you know what I mean."

"How?" the little queen asked. She was getting very excited. This could be *the answer*.

"Well," the string woman said, "when one goes from not walking to walking or not sleeping to sleeping, one feels and knows and senses a transition and the resulting action, and one feels one knows it well, better than if there had not been the not walking or not sleeping."

"That makes sense," the little queen agreed.

The string woman nodded, agreeing with herself. "But most of us cannot not live and live, at least that I know of, so maybe the next best thing is to ponder not living and then to live," she said.

"That also makes sense," the little queen said.

"I myself take a moment each day to think about my impending death," the string woman said.

"That may do the trick," the little queen said, though she was not quite sure. She wanted to live in the best way possible, and perhaps pondering her impending death would help with this. Even if it did not, she would try. She was sorry she should have to part ways with the string woman. It was like she had found a new friend.

"Won't you join me on my journey?" the string woman asked.

Yes, the little queen realized, *she would love to*. And so she said so.

The little queen walked with the string woman for what she thought would only be a short distance, yet it turned out to be much longer. In fact, she forgot all about her palace. She enjoyed walking with her friend, for it opened her up in a magnificent and tumultuous way. Each day she and the string woman thought about their impending deaths. The little queen even painted and sang a bit.

Many joined them, so the little queen met some lovely folk. They traveled to the smallest towns and the largest cities, and crossed green pastures and turquoise lakes and the sandiest of deserts. They passed through deep seas and crossed high peaks, and journeyed through the jungliest of jungles and the marshiest of marshes. They edged their way along rivers and streams, not to mention through a tunnel or two.

The little queen also began writing rose petal poems. She wrote them by night and gave them away at first light. The poems came to her like thoughts. Writing them, she thought of all those she had met. Holding them, they felt like little lives and loves in her hands. Giving them away, the little queen was pleased it seemed they floated into open arms. People read her poems and passed them on.

The little queen considered looking for the rose petal poet to see if she might like to trade places with her as the little queen, but then realized she would like to continue being the little queen. She could be many things as the little queen, including a rose petal poet.

In time, the little queen had traveled around the globe, and she was glad to arrive back in her kingdom. The string woman would go on.

The little queen shed many tears for her friend and the string woman cried too. The little queen wrote a note for the very last section of the string woman's string, for this was what all those who were touched by her did, weighing her string in place—or at least as in place as one could place a string that wrapped around the world.

The little queen's note told the string woman that she loved her, for she was too shy to say so aloud. But when the string woman read her note, she hugged the little queen and whispered into her ear that she loved the little queen too.

- XIII -

Wherein the little queen
joins a board of directors

The little queen once again found herself standing before her kingdom's library. It was good to be back. This time, she had a mission: she wanted to leave a few things for the archives.

When the little queen entered the orb of library light, she once again let the dark cool of the books embrace her. She passed the book sniffer and wall sawyer and nodded to them as they worked away in a quiet, dusty frenzy. When she reached the library archives, she handed over a selection of treasured findings from her adventures with the string woman: a few leaves, a bit of sky, some songs, a bottle of earth, and a poem. When this was done, she smiled in relief.

Exiting the library, the little queen paused to sit beside a beautiful nude statue and to decide what to do next. She would like a bit of rest. She smiled, thinking back on things—and the statue smiled back. She blinked—and the statue blinked as well. Blink, blink. The little queen peered at the figure more closely . . .

The thinker sat on a pedestal demonstrating what it is to think. Once someone had asked if she really thought as she sat apparently thinking, and she had to admit that most of the time she tried to avoid it. But after this, she made a concentrated effort to think on a daily basis. It was not so bad after all, so she decided to make it the occasional hobby.

The little queen found herself enamored by the thinker. She thought it must be difficult to try to think as one tried to look like one was thinking, for how could one think anything except for how one ought to be? As the little queen observed the thinker in admiration, another patron laughed, "Oah hah hah!"

"Why are you laughing?" the little queen asked. She already felt fondness for the thinker in their shared smiles and blinks.

"I apologize! I was not laughing at anyone," the laugher said. "There are moments before, during, and after laughter in which you do not think at all," she explained. She laughed then, and it was wide open like the echo of a ripe melon. "Heh! Heh!" The laugher thought it safest to admit she was happy in the midst of laughter, that there was nothing better than to be a laughing being, her diaphragm a big melon.

The thinker nodded. "A laugh or a thought must be given its proper space to breathe. Sometimes the best thoughts arrive without thinking at all," she said.

The little queen nodded as well, for she had found this true while walking.

"The best laughs come without thoughts weighing them down," the laugher said. "Laughing, I exist in my body," she said, sweeping her hands down her side. The little queen felt her laughing presence.

Suddenly, an idea occurred to the thinker. "We ought to begin a school that teaches individuals how to go about laughing and thinking."

"Yes," the laugher agreed. "Though I never liked school."

"Oh, well, I learned a few things there," the thinker said slowly.

"How about a school that teaches pupils how *not* to think," the laugher said. "Schools nowadays have it all backward."

"I am not sure about that," the thinker said. "It is good to know how to think about a thing or two, if you know what I mean."

"Well, we must offer a course on how to take

a bath and how to take a breath," the laugher said.

Something occurred to the little queen. "Also, a course on the ways in which one may wake— the stillness, the dreams, the movements," she suggested. As she spoke, she thought of the tree woman's limbs, the dream writer's dreams, and her journey with the string woman.

Her companions nodded. "A course on melodic conversation would also be useful. People nowadays do not know how to place a pause," the laugher said.

"What would the school be called?" the thinker asked. "Names and words and such were always hard for me."

"Maybe it can be a school without a name," the laugher suggested.

The thinker shook her head. "A nice idea, but I am afraid no one would know about it."

"We could call it the Teaching School for now," the little queen said.

"Yes!" the laugher and the thinker agreed.

"I would be happy to be on the board of directors," the little queen said. The thinker and the laugher smiled and laughed in agreement, and they all had their first meeting that very day.

- XIV -

*Wherein the little queen feels an infinite ache
and offers the sound of her smile*

The little queen was very close to home.
Now, she wanted to visit her mother and father,
for she had not been back for a long while.

The little queen loved the palace graveyard,
nestled into a hidden spot on her hill, for it was
a place of many growing things, with rolling
mounds of moss and trellises of roses and old
oaks covered in ivy. Here, wandering, one might
spot a dream in a leaf. The little queen realized
now that all these growing things offered lots of
windows of light and wondrous worlds where
one could slip into a thought, a place of peace.

When the little queen reached the graveyard,
she let her toes sink into the earth. She

considered the many bodies of land and water she had touched with these same feet.

When she came to the graves of her mother and father, both enveloped by more roses than before, she paused for a moment, felt the shiver of a breeze, an infinite ache, then continued on.

Walking on, the little queen found herself on another hill near a pond.

Saw a woman lying on a large stone lit with what remained of the day's sun.

Thought to approach the woman and wondered if she should not.

But then the woman turned her head and smiled at the little queen.

It was the editor of the Digital Dictionary of Sounds.

The little queen recognized her immediately. The woman was famous for her very large ears. The editor of the Digital Dictionary of Sounds would go anywhere for her sounds, and that included palace graveyards. At this particular moment, she happened to be wondering if sunshine made a sound as the rays hit the rocks.

The little queen stepped toward the sunlit stone. "I am a great fan of your sounds and often listen to them before going to sleep," she said.

"Oh, thank you, I so appreciate that," the woman replied with a smile.

"You may be interested to hear that I know of bodily sounds perhaps previously undiscovered," the little queen said provocatively.

"Really!" the editor of the Digital Dictionary of Sounds said, drawing out her recorder. The recorder was even larger than her ears.

The little queen nodded. "The sound of a smile, for instance."

"Tell me more! Do all people make a sound when they smile? Is it like a fingerprint? Can you smile for me?" the editor of the Digital Dictionary of Sounds asked. She placed the recorder to the cherubic left cheek of the little queen.

"I can only speak for myself, but it does seem like most people make a sound when they smile," the little queen said.

"Let us see—or rather, hear—the smile, now!" the editor said with an eagerness bordering on impatience.

The little queen created a smile, slowly but surely, and the editor of the Digital Dictionary of Sounds leaned forward.

"Do you hear anything?" the little queen asked. She smiled again, slowly.

The editor frowned. "A whispering flow of saliva? A crinkling of sorts within the tissues of the skin? A movement of the ears or rearrangement of the hair?" she offered.

"I may have some helpful devices at my palace," the little queen offered.

"Thank you, I will definitely listen to your smile more closely and probably come to you for assistance," the editor of the Digital Dictionary of Sounds said.

The little queen nodded. "You may also be interested in recording a withheld fart, but I cannot do that one on command," she said.

The editor of the Digital Dictionary of Sounds laughed. The little queen thought she looked splendid there, sitting on her rock. The little queen liked her kindly way and was surprised to realize she already felt a fondness forming. "How did you come to be so?" she asked, for she found that her companion was just so, in the best way one could be.

"Well," the editor of the Digital Dictionary of Sounds began.

The little queen noticed that each sound that came from her mouth was a work of art in a way, a kind of sweet gold key that crept inside her being.

"Once a seer surveyed my ears and said they were a very lucky pair," the editor of the Digital Dictionary of Sounds said. "They were indeed uncommonly large, like those of my great-great-grandfather."

The little queen nodded, though for some reason she had a difficult time comprehending the meaning behind the woman's words. At a distance, the little queen had been so focused on her ears that she had not noticed her beautiful brown eyes.

This is what the editor of the Digital Dictionary of Sounds explained:

As she and her ears grew older, she began finding sounds in hidden spots—the tumbling, whooshing echo of a falling rock, the susurrus collapse of a spider's web, the rot of wood rubbed by the sun. She tried to gather pastoral sounds in *Volume I*. *Volume II* included sounds of human flesh—the bodily sounds of digestion and respiration, languages and laughter, the whistle and song, and so on. *Volume III* explored the merging of natural and manmade sounds, like rain dinning on tin roofs.

The little queen nodded, and the editor of the Digital Dictionary of Sounds laughed, for she was glad to have a listener even if that listener was not completely listening. A pair of ears was always something special to the editor of the Digital Dictionary of Sounds, and she quite liked those of the little queen. The little queen had very little ears, but already they held a special place in the woman's heart.

The little queen took a seat on the stone beside the editor of the Digital Dictionary of Sounds. Each of them admired the other's ears and eyes and smiles, and in that moment both of them knew that they had fallen in love.

In the coming weeks, the little queen felt something joyous and secret floating about in her heart as she went about her days with the editor of the Digital Dictionary of Sounds. It was like her heart was alert to something no one knew, including herself. It was like she was living a lovely, long breath. The little queen felt she was a kind of strange echo of all things for the editor of the Digital Dictionary of Sounds, and the editor of the Digital Dictionary of Sounds felt this as well, for neither could ever tire of the other.

But as much as she loved the editor of the Digital Dictionary of Sounds and could lay about makings sounds with her all day, the little queen wanted to experience more of the world. Circling the world with the string woman had not been enough. The editor of the Digital Dictionary of Sounds had traveled the world many times over and wanted to continue working with her collected sounds to compile them into a *Volume IV*. They understood that they must part.

"I will keep my ears open for you," the little queen said. And so the two kissed each other goodbye and cried and knew they would see each other again. The editor of the Digital Dictionary of Sounds would remain at the palace to watch over things while the little queen was gone.

- XV -

Wherein the little queen embarks on a third
adventure with great determination

The little queen surrendered herself to serendipity, eager to be swept off her feet and into an ocean of the might, may, and could.

After a long voyage overseas and longer days thinking about her newfound love, the little queen reached an immense land immersed in language, a land with things bigger than she had ever seen. When she arrived at shore, she was really arriving at the base of a mountain. At the base of this mountain was the hummer.

Looking at the hummer beside the mountain, the little queen saw a close resemblance. The hummer stood, tall and still and spacious, hums emanating outward, her body filled with sound. Standing on this unknown land, the little queen felt how the hummer could ever so gently embrace a person with her hums. Her hums filled the little queen up so she did not feel lost or lonely.

The hummer specialized in hums and thought it strange how others liked to flap their tongues. A hum would always be enough. Her hums soothed beating hearts and heated lungs where words would not. Others wondered how she lived her life in hums, but she went on and on and on. The hummer wrote an alphabet of hums and hoped to speak the Hum without a thought. She practiced humming each day and hoped to teach the Hum to others, hum by hum. She wanted conversations held in hums in every home, an orchestra of hums where words were not enough. A language of the nose and of the feeling of a thought.

"It is good to be in harmony with a hum," the hummer said to the little queen as she approached. The two sat together at the base of the mountain.

"Yes," the little queen agreed rather absently. She was thinking about telling the editor of the Digital Dictionary of Sounds how she had found the hummer.

"A story of hums can be marvelous—one glorious unified movement of language," the hummer said. The little queen thought for a moment. "You have stories composed of words composed of letters composed of hums!" she exclaimed.

The hummer nodded with an affirmative hum, then added, "But sometimes one abbreviates hums, so the Hum can be difficult to pick up."

"I would love to learn a hum or two," the little queen said.

"Alright, let us start with the letter *a*," the hummer said. "Hmmmm."

The little queen imitated the hummer. "Hmmmm."

"Again?" the hummer requested.

"Hmmmm," the little queen hummed.

"Good!" the hummer said, looking pleased. "I hope to pass the Hum on to my children so it comes naturally to them, but it would be wonderful to have disciples so the Hum spreads more quickly. The Hum is necessary in these trying times. Hm hmmmm hmmmmmmm hm hmmmm hmmm hm hmm hmmmmm," she added.

The little queen smiled, saying, "I would love for you to introduce the Hum to my kingdom."

"Thank you!" the hummer said.

The little queen nodded and let the hummer

hum on. As she looked back, it seemed that the hummer blended in with her mountain almost perfectly. She wondered what the hummer had meant by "these trying times." Maybe hummers knew things others did not.

Now, it must be noted that the little queen encountered lots of folk along her journeys, many of whom are not included here. For example, the fish talker and the fish rescuer, to name a few. But one cannot not mention the tree masseuse, for the tree masseuse blended in with her tree just as the hummer blended in with her mountain.

The tree masseuse ran her hands over the bark of trees, smooth as the sea and rough as the earth. She climbed and laddered along, rubbed and squeezed and pounded, never losing rhythm on her way. She pondered how the trees might feel, her hands a spot of warmth, like a golden sun that slowly moves through water and soil, soft and deep. She would never say they groaned, but at times it felt they released a certain bulge to breathe more easily. At the moment, the trees felt tough and tense, and the tree masseuse did not see the little queen.

As the little queen observed, she wondered

if the tree masseuse had ever massaged the tree woman. She would have to introduce them. But she did not want to interrupt the massage, so left a message for the tree masseuse at the base of her tree. The little queen was finding that a conversation could take many forms.

- XVI -

Wherein the little queen has
a frighteningly ecstatic realization

The little queen came to one of the most ancient hills in the world. It was renowned because the text shouter lived on it.

The text shouter shouted books aloud to gauge their sound and rarely wandered down her hill. Manuscripts in hand, she stood atop the hill on open ground and let the words come out in shouts to see where they would land. Sentences could fall apart and tremble in her hands. Some words held together as one cohesive clump, while others drifted off. Residents nearby were proud to have her there. Many loved to listen through their windows for the next great work, and some folks stood about outside to listen to her with their morning cups of tea.

The little queen was not the only one listening to the text shouter. The text copier biographer's consultant was also there.

The text copier biographer's consultant made her living writing out the works of writers past. Her life seemed to rest in inflections found in words, their order, and something more. She said that you could know someone by what they wanted of their words in the world and what it seemed they kept from sight. Success to her was the glorious ache of a moment's rest in another's life. She hoped to reconstruct precisely vaguely a time and a space, a writer in dimension. There was nothing formulaic but for a feeling—a feeling passed to biographers in more printed words, in references to text and world.

The text copier biographer's consultant approached the text shouter as she completed the shouting of a manuscript. "A shout can make a fine mess," she said.

"A shout is a vulnerable thing. It can speak of questions and happenings that simply spoken words cannot," the text shouter said. Indeed, she felt that her shouts were a little strange these days. "When was the last time you let out a shout?"

The text copier biographer's consultant— along with the little queen—thought back and could not remember the last time she had shouted.

"Ah ha!" the text shouter shouted. "I like latitudinality, and you can get that with a shout. I ought to teach you both to shout aloud," she said. So the text shouter led the little queen and the text copier biographer's consultant to the center of her hill. Then she made a shout.

Her audience smothered their ears. Even the shout's echoes did something to the sides of the head. The little queen experienced a passing concern for her cochleas when she realized that the text copier biographer's consultant was being called upon to shout. Then it would be her turn.

The text copier biographer's consultant made a shout, but nothing seemed to come out.

"Try again!" the text shouter shouted.

And so she tried again (and again). Finally, sound came rolling out. She shouted so much, in fact, that the text shouter stuck a manuscript in her hands so she could shout even more. As she was shouting, the little queen envisioned her as a text copier-shouter biographer's consultant.

Then it was the little queen's turn. The little queen stepped up to the platform, wondering just how powerful her little body could be. She thought of her mother and father and what they might say if they could see her now. She took deep breaths and exhaled shuddering sighs. She wondered if she was capable of producing a shout. And then she breathed in again and let the air residing in her body pour out. The little queen's body shuddered with her first shout, letting her tears leave her in another sort of way. Her shouts became louder and louder as she went on, and the echoes enveloped her so it was as if many others stood by her side, always there for her if she failed to deliver the next shout. The little queen had the frighteningly ecstatic realization that she was there for herself.

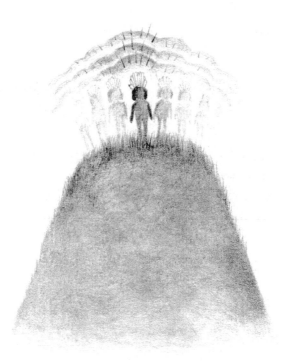

XVII

Wherein the little queen
discovers more foreign languages

As exciting as it was to shout, the little queen missed the editor of the Digital Dictionary of Sounds. She knew, though, that the realization of oneself only makes it easier to realize the possibilities that come with being beside another. So she ploughed on.

The little queen did not have to linger long to meet other interesting folks. The text shouter was so well-known she drew many wordish people to the hills around her. In a matter of days, the little queen stumbled upon the bodily linguist deep within a cave.

The bodily linguist had thought to write a language of the body, the best and sweetest bodily language there could be. It would be a language of gently squeezed eyes and hidden teeth, little hops and circling feet, softly said fricatives and humming nasals, clicking consonants and whispering whistles, inhaled breaths and released sighs, slippery snaps and echoing claps, tapping feet and undulating arms, wiggling fingers and curving necks, swaying bodies and panning eyes. The bodily linguist would dance in place ejecting language in lilting lines of sound and motion. She found that people loved her language, though it traveled slowly. It was a language best learned in person.

The little queen was, of course, not the only one interested in the bodily linguist.

The bodily linguist was trying to make up her mind as to whether A Wiggle of the Left Pinky Finger should follow A Two-Legged Hop in the sentence she was hoping to compose when the mathematical linguist came meandering along.

"I would love to learn the Bodily Language," the mathematical linguist said.

"Me too," said the little queen.

"The Bodily Language may only be taught from one to another," the bodily linguist said. "If it is written, it is long and rather indecipherable," she said. "Only one person can enact the language at once, so this is a language with few interruptions, a language that flows along," the bodily linguist went on, gyrating in place. "Sometimes a thought can only find expression in a gesture, and that is when the Bodily Language is truly experiential, for it has the potential to combine the metaphor of dance with the more precise nature of the word," she concluded with a well-placed pirouette.

As the mathematical linguist nodded, the little queen thought how she would love to introduce the Bodily Language to her kingdom.

"The Bodily Language seems a kind of dancing language," the mathematical linguist observed. The mathematical linguist strove to form a language that some hoped would birth the mathematicians of the future. A language of elision, case, and arbitrary sign, a language that, when spoken, was not always so written. A language full of multitudes of ways to form thought, where one would almost always find oneself lost. A language that could waltz or trot or meander—like a Sunday afternoon in the park. A language that could see a long ways off. The more she worked, the more the mathematical linguist found that a mathematical mind was shaped as much by the scribble on the page or simple waves of sound—what is also known as art.

The little queen listened in admiration. She told these two new friends that as exceptional persons they both were more than welcome to immigrate to her kingdom if they ever felt the inclination. No lottery would be necessary.

"Thank you, I will soon come, for I think I may need a little queen," the bodily linguist said with a strangely dangerous wink. She hopped, moved her left pinky finger, and smiled.

With that, the little queen decided it was *almost* time to return home.

XVIII

Wherein the little queen
seeks a gift in the Jungles

In the little queen's kingdom, it was customary to bring a gift to one's loved ones after a long journey. And so the little queen very much wanted to find the perfect gift for the editor of the Digital Dictionary of Sounds. When she came upon the Jungles, she knew she'd find something marvelous. Stepping into the green, she imagined the editor of the Digital Dictionary of Sounds gasping with delight.

The little queen did not know it, but the architect of chaos had shaped the Jungles into what they were.

The architect of chaos had first realized the benefits of chaos as a child. Entering a room, she found it surprising she could distinguish the snowy head of her mother from the rounded mounds of paper. Indeed, the room was a hilly landscape of ruffling sheets of text, each one contributing to the overall effect. Sitting down, she found herself agreeably comfortable, felt a productive energy gleaned from chaos—she could see the white sheets flowering into lilies.

Finding herself overflowing with the chaotic, she did not feel the need to create order.

Ever since, the architect of chaos had striven to construct the most perfect chaos. The most perfect chaos ought to be contained in order to be experienced to the fullest, to create an intense combustion of that containment. The most perfect chaos ought to be a quiet and difficult chaos, to lend further tension to the tumult, to tense upon a person with the utmost civility— something like a softly boiling landscape.

Though the little queen did not know the story of the architect of chaos, she could sense that story infused in the landscape itself. She felt a curious vibration deep within herself and felt at one with the chaos around her.

The little queen decided simply to go into the heart of the Jungles, for in her travels she had learned that one ought always to simply go to the heart of things. This is how she found the seasons collector.

The seasons collector had rows of rounded jars, ceramic jars, and short and tall and wide glass jars, jars the size of teardrops, and even one colossal jar the size of a cottage house. She had jars as thin as petals and jars as thick as arms. Spring or summer, fall or winter, she would not fail to take a jar, collect a bit of air, and keep her wares until they might be wanted. With a thin black pen, she marked the date, the time, and the temperature upon the lid of each jar, then placed it in its space in a quiet barn, on wide oak shelves. The jars were her babes, each an age and each with a heartbeat. Those who suffered heat or cold lined up to buy a jar, liked to feel the seasons at their fingertips, and lovers would exchange the jars to mark their anniversaries.

"You have just what I need," the little queen said.

The seasons collector smiled. "Would you like to try one from last week?" she asked. She handed a walnut-sized jar to the little queen.

"Thank you."

"You may use it anytime, anywhere," the seasons collector said.

The little queen looked at the label on the jar: "The Last Days of Summer." Then she opened it.

What a feeling! A heartbeat! A tinkling! Inchoation upon inchoation of sensation relived!

"You give chaos shape and make the moment tremble," the little queen said.

"You make it all sound very exciting," the seasons collector laughed.

"May I have one jar of each of the four seasons in the past year?" asked the little queen. She knew that the editor of the Digital Dictionary of Sounds would like to compare the sounds of the seasons.

"As you wish," the seasons collector said, placing the jars in a box.

"Thank you!" the little queen said. Then she went on her way. It was time to return home. And then the Happening happened.

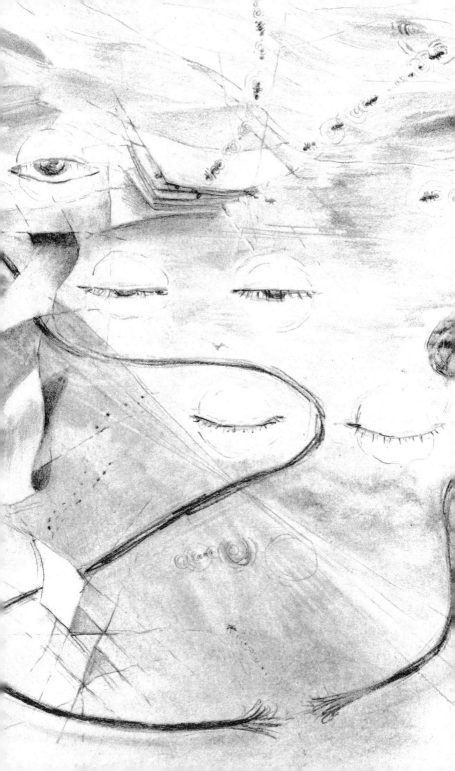

- XIX -

Wherein the Happening happens

The book sniffer was releasing a sniff of good book. The wall sawyer was making space. The tree woman was adjusting a limb. The leaf gluer was manipulating the tips of a leaf. The seasons painter was standing beneath a tree. The creature sweeper was eyeing a stubborn ant. The street painter was on a road in the sea. The animal singer was singing to herself. The fish talker was blinking. The fish rescuer was rescuing. The dream writer was recording a dream. The dream counter was forgetting. The window builder was wondering if oceans were windows. The window counter was wondering if all windows reflect. The lotioner was spilling. The plant whisperer was practicing voice vibrations. The perfumer was sniffing. The foreshadowing artist was sharpening. The sleep soother was trying not to fall asleep. The poop encourager was dreaming of shapes. The maker of long books was leading a long book race. The string woman was tying her eighth string around the world. The thinker was thinking about thinking. The laugher was lying in bed.

The editor of the Digital Dictionary of Sounds was closing her eyes. The hummer was listening to a mountain. The tree masseuse was gauging the firmness of a branch. The text shouter was swaying in shouts. The text copier biographer's consultant was leaning. The bodily linguist was learning to tap dance. The mathematical linguist was drawing signs in sand. The architect of chaos was simmering in paper. The seasons collector was tightening a jar. It came without warning and was over in a series of moments. Books caved   spaces filled   l i m b s c o l l a p s e d leaves flew   trees fell ants ran roads cracked song stopped   eyes shut   r e s c u e s ended   dreams paused   thoughts tangled oceans shuddered   w i n d o w s s p l i t lotion melted   voices cried   p e r f u m e s popped   pencils disintegrated   sleep woke   poop thinned   r a c e s e n d e d string broke   t h o u g h t s q u i v e r e d beds stilled   eyes expired   m o u n t a i n s screeched   branches shivered   h i l l s moved   shelves shook   shoes expanded s a n d contracted   paper folded   j a r s b u r s t—a shifting of sky, earth, and sea, a rending gesture of wind, a drifting.

Wherein the little queen wanders and walks

The little queen wandered, lost. She moved through broken trees and sat by several seas. She came across those whose homes were gone, and their wails hurt her heart. She held onto her leaf, brush, string, jars. She saw birds who had lost their song. She walked day and night through collapsed kingdoms and saw how many bodies needed homes. She did not want to think of what might have befallen her people or her love.

The little queen walked on for months. She made her way in the direction of home thinking that the editor of the Digital Dictionary of Sounds, who had not seen her for a long while, probably thought she was gone. She knew that those who knew there was a little queen likely believed she had passed with the Happening. Anyway, no one really knew what a little queen could do to help with something like this.

The little queen had found that walking could bring ideas, though. As she walked, she had a few of them. She began to walk intentionally. She gathered roses and made a pile of petals.

She took a needle in hand, sitting in the sun and rain for long hours. And soon she began to distribute rose petal posts on her way home.

- XXI -

Wherein the little queen
reflects in the Wild Rose Gardens

As the little queen distributed her posts, she thought about those she loved. Maybe this is what led her, finally, to the Wild Rose Gardens. And, too, the need to gather more petals. Here she could sit for a brief moment and work. Her little legs did hurt.

The little queen had spent much time as a child in the Wild Rose Gardens, a place many days away from the palace, but not so distant as the lands of language. The gardens were full of memories. They had arches, benches, and mossy patches of various sizes as one went along, so they had the layering and texture of something grander than themselves.

The little queen felt at home, here. She felt the presence of love. Whenever she felt at home, there always seemed to be love floating about on the edges of things. She remembered running along these dirt paths, stumbling upon her mother and father exchanging a kiss. She recalled licking a rose because she wanted to know if it tasted as good as it smelled. Once she had fallen into a rose bush and no one was around to help. While the thorns had been painful, the memories of rose petal baths and gentle embraces far exceeded any scars.

The Wild Rose Gardens had been constructed by the architect of solitude, who strove to construct the most perfect solitude. After much experimentation, the architect of solitude had concluded that the most perfect solitude must verge on its opposite, company. The most perfect solitude must not allow infiltration by any sound. The most perfect solitude must stand like a stone cathedral, still and beautiful and impenetrable; it must be so heavy in its presence that one feels its tightening around the waist, its weight upon the shoulders. The most perfect solitude must entail the absence of all beings, but it must also tremble with the light of life. For example, a perfect solitude may find itself haunted by lives born of the imagination, characters lying on shelves in rows of books, or accompanied by figures waiting in dreams. The perfect solitude pushes one to sense the pulse of solitude itself; for example, a perfect solitude may be marked with the beat of one's heart.

The little queen did not know any of this, but she felt it in her being, and that was enough. She thought it peculiar that the lands of an architect of chaos and an architect of solitude felt so similar, though she did not have the terminology to put these thoughts into words. Sitting, she became a part of solitude itself. Memories of her mother and father enhanced this perfect solitude. As she was thinking of how her mother smiled, her face lifting and opening like the secret blossoming of a flower at night, the little queen felt a big fragrant rose upon her face. All of a sudden, she realized she felt like kissing roses.

The little queen got up from her rose petal posts and kissed this big fragrant rose. Then she rose from her bench to kiss another and proceeded to kiss another and another, for there was always one more . . . She gathered them up in her arms, and it was like gathering a great bouquet of kisses. It made her think of holding the world in her arms. She stood still, letting the sun pour into her body. She felt a vibrating, a delicate trembling. And she knew, no matter what, she would have much to hold onto.

(This was when the reflector appeared, of course. The reflector's hair was like a cloud that seemed about to burst, her body full of curves. Those who looked at her looked into her depths and saw themselves in fragments. Sometimes someone wanted her to come a little closer, but other times they wished for her to leave, for mirrors are not always pleasant things. She never spoke, but simply magnified the lives of those whom she approached.

The little queen looked for a while at the reflector, who had appeared in a twinkle and tinkle of mirror bits with her spoon shoes.

"Reflection offers ideal solitude," the little queen observed.

The reflector did not say a word.

"The moment seduces itself," the little queen said.

The reflector still did not speak.

The little queen peered into the reflector's mirrors. "I am here and I am there and there and there and possibly, potentially everywhere," the little queen said.

The reflector twirled.

"What if I created fields of mirror in my kingdom?" the little queen asked with excitement.

The reflector looked into the distance.

"What if we reflect and reflect to create a revolution of reflection where everyone sees themselves and everything else, really sees the possibilities?" the little queen asked.

The reflector walked away.

The little queen thought it had been a very nice exchange overall even if it had only been with herself.)

Wherein the little queen
makes use of a little piece of string

The little queen thought about the editor of the Digital Dictionary of Sounds. Of how the two of them were a kind of echo of all things for one another, of how their echoes made new sound. How dearly she hoped her love was alive.

The little queen returned to half a palace on a hill of lavender soaked in dew drops lit by the sun.

She found the editor of the Digital Dictionary of Sounds sitting by the same window that she had once sat at, as if waiting for a miracle. The large ears of the editor of the Digital Dictionary of Sounds made a shadow across her face.

"Who is it?" the editor of the Digital Dictionary of Sounds asked.

The little queen took a step toward her love, clutching the jars of seasons in her arms. They had traveled a long way and her little hands shook.

The eyes of the editor of the Digital Dictionary of Sounds were closed, but her eyelids fluttered.

It was as if she was trying to see, but could not. "Who are you?" she asked.

"I am no one of consequence," the little queen said.

A tear fell down the cheek of the editor of the Digital Dictionary of Sounds. "You sound just like her, but no, it cannot be."

The little queen saw that her editor held a jar of tears close to her heart. "I want to give you these," the little queen said, replacing the jar of tears with the jars of the seasons collector.

The editor of the Digital Dictionary of Sounds nodded in thanks, holding the jars tightly in her arms. More tears escaped, and the little queen could no longer bear her little game. She began shedding tears as well.

Her love heard them rolling down her cheeks. "Will you tell me who you happen to be, as I cannot see and it seems my hearing is also impaired?" asked the editor of the Digital Dictionary of Sounds.

The little queen took the hands of her love. "I am little and I am yours if you will marry me," she said.

"My dear little queen," the editor of the Digital Dictionary of Sounds whispered.

"What do you say?" the little queen said, for she thought she knew the answer, but one can never be sure in these things.

"Yes, as long as I do not have to be a little queen," the editor of the Digital Dictionary of Sounds said.

The little queen laughed delightedly.

And so it was.

The little queen called on the friends she had made on her adventures, as well as those whom she had only heard of but felt were friends already. She invited them to her lavender hill for the wedding.

All responded—they already were on their way because of her rose petal post: an announcement asking them to present themselves.

It was an occasion to remember.

The little queen and the editor of the Digital Dictionary of Sounds walked down the aisle together to songs of their favorite sounds, down a little lane lined with books and roses and the sweetest scents.

Standing beneath a tree wearing leaf crowns, they spoke of dreams and exchanged rings made from a treasured piece of string.

It was a simple ceremony, and the little queen knew her mother and father would be happy for her, to see that she had found someone even if that someone had big ears and was blind.

- XXIII -

*Wherein the little queen and her friends
make homes for those in need*

The little queen did not forget about the Happening. She asked her friends to look inside themselves and to look around. To see the windows that wanted to be seen and the folks who needed sleep or song. To sweep paths and streets and strings into the future. To make homes for those in need, for those displaced by the Happening. "A home is a resting place for the heart," the little queen said. And that is how the little queen and her many friends healed their world.

The book sniffer, the wall sawyer, the tree woman, and the leaf gluer built the Open Home of Books and Leaves. It was a barn full of bookshelves, and mounds of books warm with the gentle smell of hay. A house stitched of books with windows of page. An open place without walls where light and air could dance in the mornings and evenings. Sun pouring in on wave upon wave of cooling dew. Curtains of leaves that swayed and shimmered between rooms.

Beds of leaves for sleeping. Walls enmeshed in leafy veins of deepening reds, oranges, and greens. A home open to birds needing rest from the rain. A home where limbs could be in absolute stillness. A home that gathered and released dust in long and lovely breaths.

The seasons painter, the creature sweeper, the street painter, and the animal singer designed the Colorful Home of Creatures and Song, a home of wood on land, a warm, shadowed space, as if brushed into tremulous being. Each room awash in a different color: cerise, mandarin, forsythia, argyle, gulfstream, danube, and framboise. Every room a mood depending on the falling light, the shade, the time of day. Halls of rainbow roads imagined in measured strokes. Floors of earth imprinted with hooves and paws and feet and other trails of breathing beings. Painted stairways lined with tangled roses and ivy. A room covered in canvas. A room filled only with stair. Hanging brushes and brooms. Branches crossing in shadow above doorways—a palace for birds to roost, in a way. Creatures swaying to a voice drifting through glassless windows between rooms.

The dream writer, the dream counter, the

fish talker, and the fish rescuer designed the Dreamy Home of Water and Hammocks, a home nestled in the sea, made of glass walls. Stories and dreams scribbled on walls for passing fish who cared to read. A home of watching and listening. A saltwater pool in which one could swim with fish and coral and turtles and other creatures of the deep. Knobby and sloping stairways of driftwood and shell. Beds of sand and seaweed. Dreams that floated about like trickling thoughts waiting to be scooped up. A home filled with hammocks that swayed in an imagined breeze, the only kind of wind a wave. A home where one could melt into a thought, a motion, the curving moment of a dream.

The window builder, the window counter, the lotioner, and the plant whisperer designed the Windowy Home of Greens and Release, a home that hinted at memory and its possibility. Windows always waiting to be built into translucent existence. Different degrees of sunshine, different designs beaming through. A home of many worlds. Windows of glass or simply wooden frame, of screen and growing things. The softness of windows offset by stone floors, floors offering whispers a chance to murmur to wakefulness and awaken other beings. Greenhouse rooms full of sage, rosemary, aloe vera. A home in constant and quiet birth.

The perfumer, the foreshadowing artist, the sleep soother, and the poop encourager designed the Fragrant Home of Pencils and Pens, a home of earthly tunnels. Thousands of round little holes in each room's walls for pencils and pens to rest. A home where one could trace one's route with one's nose. A home so lit that one would wonder where one was. A home where one always felt she was returning to something like scribbles on the page. The scents of the world shifting in subtle ways. Soft and sharp smells that displaced. Rooms of empty jars awaiting perfumes and paint. Lavender-lined doorways and beds. A home nestled into itself like the bowels of the earth. Narrow paths so that one moved and breathed slowly, careful not to rupture others' ways. A home of many-tunneled floors with a lower trapdoor. A home with rooms so dark they would always remain unknown.

The maker of long books, the string woman, the thinker, and the laugher designed the

Drifting Home of Movement and Moments, a home of body and mind, where one might travel or sit in one place for long amounts of time. A miniature lake with a dozen floating boats full of books. Pages hung from walls, flowed from ceilings. Rooms of hidden panels awaiting discovery. Halls in which one might write a passing thought to mark time, golden floors covered in messages and letters. A room in which one must always laugh in order to pass through. A porch with a bubble blower nestled on its railing. A home one might leave in peace in order to do other things, a home that would maybe drift a bit, but would mostly stay in place.

The little queen, the editor of the Digital Dictionary of Sounds, the hummer, and the tree masseuse designed the Growing Home of Silence and Sound, a home with the deepening beauty of a tree over time. A home that made no sound, merged and fell with the pouring rain. Walls as thick as a sequoia's and walls that could shed like a birch. Walls of trees and growing things, all ready to expand with the touch of a hand. Rooms full of noise and rooms full of living silence. A humming room of recordings.

Air that could expand a silence or a sound. Stairways leading to doorways leading to open space. Bathtubs of water lilies. Little drums in the corner of a room. The home's solid skeleton ready to be gently touched, every step a moment that opened and closed, like a treasure box.

The text shouter, the text copier biographer's consultant, the bodily linguist, and the mathematical linguist designed the Textual Home of Body and Language, a home on a hill with roomfuls of text and letters. A roof with the circular curve of a *c* and doors with the solid opening of an *o* and walls with the steady standing of a *t* and spiraling banisters with the sliding surface of *s*. A home a little too inside itself, but a home with a rooftop from which one could yell. Windows overflowing with words. A home that could be erected or wrecked by a word. Rooms with shapes evoking a feeling in the body, each time in a slightly different place. Open floors prompting handstands and somersaults. Gesturing portraits and spinning clocks that made one dizzy.

And finally, the architect of solitude, the reflector, the architect of chaos, and the seasons collector built the Pulsing Home of Mirrors and

Music, a home like a heart in the womb of the sea. A home abreast in the whoosh and slap of wind and water. A boat with a space below deck to rest in the solitude of sea for a time. A room full of mirrors—mirrors of every size and shape so one might choose a mirror for each day. A home always looking at itself like the sky in the sea. A home trembling and rocking with water and earth, the cleanest chaos of seaweed and saltwater washing aboard. The rushing softness of waves. A trail of collected jars kept cool in the sea. A ledger of measures like that of the solitude and chaos and energy on the air. A home ready to birth something sweet like spring.

Wherein nothing much remains to be said

Not much remains to be said. All were welcomed into the homes built by the little queen and her friends. The homes transcended the little queen's dreams, and if one seeks them in just the right way, they may be found in a heartbeat.

CPSIA information can be obtained
at www.ICGtesting.com
Printed in the USA
LVOW03s1517220218
567559LV00003B/737/P